WAITING FOR A FRIEND: A PLAY

Alfred C. Martino

WAITING FOR A FRIEND: A PLAY

Alfred C. Martino

Coles Street Publishing
Jersey City, New Jersey

www.AlfredMartino.com

Library of Congress Cataloging-in-Publication Data
Martino, Alfred C.
Waiting For A Friend: A Play / by Alfred C. Martino.
p. cm.
Summary: A fifty-something-year old man has a chance
encounter
with a best friend from his youth.
[1. Growing old-Fiction. 2. Friendship-Fiction.
3. New Jersey-Fiction. 4. Stage play-Fiction.] I. Title.
[Fic]- dc22 2011934850
ISBN 978-1-931953-99-3

Text and Cover Designed by Coles Street Publishing

First edition
ACEGHFDB

Printed in the United States of America

Alfred C. Martino is the author of the award-winning novels: Perfected By Girls, Over The End Line, and Pinned; the stage play, Waiting For A Friend; and the short stories, "Quiet Desperation," "The Date," "A Day At The Beach," "Where Am I?" "Breathing In Rio," "A Cowboy's Way," "Mother, Interrupter," "The Boy And Girl: A Parable," "Grad School Daydreams," and "I Have Never Been Murdered." Alfred is also lyricist of the goth metal song, "Curse At The Sky." Information about the author, and these titles in print, ebook, and audiobook formats, can be found at AlfredMartino.com.

WAITING FOR A FRIEND

A Play in One Act

by

Alfred C. Martino

Cast of Characters

Man   A man in his early fifties

Steven   A 15-year old high school boy, with dark,
                    uncombed hair, wearing a The Cars 1980s
                    concert T-shirt.

Scene

Outdoors, but no specific location.

Time

The present.

(AT RISE we see a MAN, down stage left, standing alone, seeming contemplative, tired, perhaps a little older than his years.)

MAN
(turns to the opposite side of the stage, where STEVEN walks in slowly, almost meandering.)
Hello, Steven.
(a beat)
Well, this is a surprise.

STEVEN
(with a slight smile)
Is it?

MAN
Yes.

STEVEN
A pleasant one?

MAN
Sure.
(gestures to The Cars T-shirt he's wearing)
God, that was a great concert. You used to wear the T-shirt all the time. Never took it off. Even with that tear on the sleeve.

STEVEN
(nodding, touching the sleeve)
How are you?

MAN
(shrugs)
Good.

STEVEN
It's been a long time.

MAN
It has.

STEVEN

How long has it been?

MAN

Well, years... Too many years.

STEVEN

How many?

MAN

How many?

STEVEN

Yeah.

MAN

Are you really asking me?

STEVEN

I am.

MAN

Does it matter?

STEVEN

It does.

MAN

I don't think so.

STEVEN

But do you know?

MAN

Of course, I know.

STEVEN

And?

MAN

Thirty-something years...
            (a beat)

Thirty-two... Thirty-three...

                        STEVEN
Which is it?

                        MAN
Thirty-five.
                  (a beat)
I guess.

                        STEVEN
                  (half-laughing)
You guess?

                        MAN
                  (takes in a deep breath, stares off in the
                  distance, then mutters.)
This isn't what I need. Not today. Not now.
                  (a long beat)
It's been thirty-five years, two months, and eleven days. But
who's counting?
                  (sighing)
A lifetime ago.

                        STEVEN
A lifetime.

                        MAN
Well, I made it to fifty. Passed the big five-oh.

                        STEVEN
Sounds like a big deal.

                        MAN
I suppose.

                        STEVEN
You're the grizzled old man with wisdom etched on his face.

                        MAN
Grizzled? Not sure about that. And the wisdom etched on my
face? It's wrinkles... Many wrinkles.

STEVEN
(snarky)
So, you're pretty much just plain old?

MAN
(almost to himself)
Hitting fifty, yeah, it means I'm old. I'd always thought so
when we were kids. Seeing my parents or my aunts and
uncles, wondering if I'd ever make it to their age. Wondering,
even more, if I wanted to make it to their age.

STEVEN
(sarcastically)
Catch you at a bad time?

MAN
(as if shaken out of his thoughts)
Not really.

STEVEN
Somewhere you have to be?

MAN
Steven, there's always somewhere I have to be. Or
something I need to be doing.

STEVEN
Don't let me keep you.

MAN
No, no, I've got some time now.

STEVEN
Seems I kind of surprised you.

MAN
Just didn't know you'd be coming by.

STEVEN
Don't you really mean, Why'm I here?

8

                    MAN
No.

                    STEVEN
No?

                    MAN
            (firmly)
No.
            (after a beat, he relents)
Okay, yes, I am wondering why.

                    STEVEN
See, that wasn't so hard.
            (a beat)
I came by to talk about stuff. Bring up some memories.
Shoot the shit a little. Know what I mean? Like that night way
back when.

                    MAN
Which night?

                    STEVEN
When we first became friends.

                    MAN
            (thinking)
Okay... sure.

                    STEVEN
You hesitated.

                    MAN
Are you testing me again?

                    STEVEN
Your words. Not mine.

                    MAN
Well, are you?

                    STEVEN

It doesn't sound like you remember. I'll give you some time to think about it.

                         MAN
No, I remember. Maybe not all of it. But enough. Ninth grade. Early October. End of an Indian summer.
                    (to himself)
The exact circumstances elude me -- who Steven and I were hanging out with that night, where we were going. Like trying to read the faint impression left after erasing pencil marks, there were fragile snippets of recollection, vague images, but none quite vivid enough to grab hold of with all of my memory.
                    (a beat)
Had the passing decades irreversibly faded such a significant night of my life? Surely, remembering the feeling of the night was most important, but trying to convince myself of that was falling decidedly short.

                        STEVEN
                    (with a smirk)
Need some help?

                         MAN
                    (irritated)
Not at all.
                    (a beat)
We ran into each other looking for a party, right? Met up with some kids from Deerfield. Ended up walking miles and miles. Down Old Short Hills Road, I think. Then across Hobart Ave towards Glenwood, probably.

                        STEVEN
                    (prodding)
Talked about the best-looking girls in school.

                         MAN
Yes... yes.

                        STEVEN
Playing on the freshman soccer team.

                              MAN
And becoming famous when we grew up -- that I do
remember.

                            STEVEN
What else?

                              MAN
What else? Is remembering every moment really necessary?
                          (a beat)
The truth is, the night you and I became friends we walked
all over Short Hills, but nowhere that I can exactly recall. We
met up with people from junior high, then left them to find
some others. We talked about everything -- everything that
meant anything -- even if the specifics elude me right now.
It's been thirty-five years, for God's sakes.
                          (a beat)
Besides, I've got the overall theme right.

                            STEVEN
Ah, but the Devil's in the details.

                              MAN
I was there. I lived it.

                            STEVEN
So did I.

                              MAN
Yes...
                          (a beat)
So did you.

                            STEVEN
But it stays in the past.

                              MAN
Is that a question?

                            STEVEN
You tell me.

                    MAN
Or a statement of the obvious?

                    STEVEN
Again, you tell me.

                    MAN
Either way, I suppose it stays in the past.
                    (a beat)
Maybe that's for the best.

                    STEVEN
Or not.

                    MAN
Or not...

                    STEVEN
                    (a beat)
That was the beginning. We hung out a lot after that night.
With Chuckie and Kenny and Preston. Riding our mopeds
around town all day. Working on the engines at night in your
garage. Listening to The Cars and...
                    (loud)
Fuckin' Van--
                    (looking to the Man to finish the phrase, but
                    he doesn't, so Steven tries again)
Fuckin' Van--

                    MAN
                    (reluctantly)
Fuckin' Halen...

                    STEVEN
                    (mimics playing instruments)
Come on. Eddie on guitar, Alex on drums. David Lee Roth
wailing... Let's try it again.
                    (loud)
Fuckin' Van!

                    MAN
                    (still reluctantly, but louder)

Fuckin' Halen.

                    STEVEN
            (nods his head in approval)
And, man, we busted chops.

                    MAN
We did a lot of that.

                    STEVEN
Called Sue and Lisa on the phone all the time. God, Lisa had
a great rack. Walked around the corner from your house to
Laura's. Never cared what time it was. Never concerned
about when to get home. We lived for the moment just
ahead of us.

                    MAN
The things we did didn't even have to be a big deal.
            (a beat)
Most of the time they were pretty ordinary.

                    STEVEN
Nothing was ordinary. Every day was different. Every
experience a new one.

                    MAN
Sure.

                    STEVEN
            (grinning)
And even when it was ordinary, it was still pretty damn good.

                    MAN
Yeah, it was.

                    STEVEN
            (grinning even wider)
And what about that water fight we had?

                    MAN
Water fight?

STEVEN

THE water fight.
>   (a beat)
The one we had that summer. At my house.
>   (a beat)
IN my house.

MAN

Christ...the goddamn water fight...
>   (to himself)
From way back in the vault of my innumerable life's
moments -- from obscure to salient, from hazy to spectacular
-- The Water Fight rushes to the front.
>   (he begins to smile)
That was not ordinary.

STEVEN

Insane.

MAN

It was wrong. Very wrong.

STEVEN

It was what made things better back then, know what I
mean?

MAN
>   (unsure)
Yeah.

STEVEN

Do you?

MAN

I guess I don't know.
>   (a beat)
Enlighten me. How do you mean, better?

STEVEN

Doing daring, crazy, insane things.

MAN

Look, Steven, I appreciate you coming by and wanting to dredge up all these fun times from the past. They were great, they really were. But that time has passed.

                              STEVEN
I'm talking about living.

                              MAN
It passed long ago.

                              STEVEN
Because you can't be wild or spontaneous now?

                              MAN
Yes, that's exactly what I mean.

                              STEVEN
Why?

                              MAN
Why?

                              STEVEN
Yeah, why?

                              MAN
Because I'm--
                    (he cuts himself off)

                              STEVEN
What?

                              MAN
                    (shakes his head in frustration)
I'm an adult.

                              STEVEN
                    (dismissive tone)
An adult.

                              MAN
I've got responsibilities.

                         STEVEN
Responsibilities.

                         MAN
Are you kidding me? I just can't do ridiculous things like that.
There are rules, and a certain kind of behavior that's
expected. At work, at home, wherever. And it's not wild or
crazy. That's not even in the realm of possibility.

                         STEVEN
You proved my point.

                         MAN
I didn't prove anything. You're being foolish.

                         STEVEN
You're being adult.
                    (a long beat, then he laughs)
Man, that water fight was memorable.

                         MAN
                    (with a laugh)
Memorable...
                    (to himself)
On that mid-August afternoon, a previously-silent garden
hose and a parentally-unattended house set the stage for
Steven and me, and our friend, Ira, to get into mischief-on-
steroids that would highlight the most bizarre afternoon of
our lives. It was impetuous, but calculated; chaotically stupid,
yet brilliantly fun; over-the-top irresponsible, and absolutely
perfect.

                         STEVEN
You guys started it.

                         MAN
I don't remember that.

                         STEVEN
Yes.

                              MAN

How?

                            STEVEN

You had water pistols.

                              MAN

Oh, right... Right.
                    (a beat)
Yes, the battle had humble beginnings.

                            STEVEN

I was working my ass off shining the chrome of my moped
exhaust. You and Ira kept shooting water at my ear. Then
my nose. And you'd laugh and laugh like girls. It was really
bugging the crap out of me.

                              MAN

But you got us back.

                            STEVEN

Oh, did I. An ambush when you least expected it. Waited
until you guys were lying on the front lawn trying to get a tan.
SWOOSH -- hit you with the hose on full-blast.

                              MAN

Then all hell broke loose.

                            STEVEN

Ira ran behind my house. I chased that little wuss. But the
hose only went so far...

                              MAN

And I found a few buckets in your garage. I filled them from
the outside faucet. And waited. And the moment you
stepped back on the driveway, I got ya.

                            STEVEN

Man, did you.

                              MAN

It was a small victory, but a victory nonetheless. So Ira and I

                               17

ran into your house, high-fiving each other. That should've been the end. We called out from a window for a ceasefire, but you ignored us.

                    STEVEN
I didn't ignore anything.

                    MAN
But somehow you didn't hear us?

                    STEVEN
Something like that.

                    MAN
              (shaking his head)
You lived with recklessness, Steven. It was your nature. I envied that. Only you would have taken The Water Fight to a level that surpassed reason and logic.

                    STEVEN
Hey, I had to get you guys back.

                    MAN
Even if it meant spraying water with the hose into the living room window?

                    STEVEN
Yeah.

                    MAN
INTO the living room window?

                    STEVEN
Yep.

                    MAN
And you HAD to bring full buckets inside too?

                    STEVEN
You guys controlled the second floor. I needed ammunition.

                    MAN

Standing here, decades later... My God, I can still feel that familiar fear that we were going to get caught.

STEVEN

It was war.

MAN

Steven, we were throwing buckets of water in your house! Buckets! Down the stairs, on the walls, in the kitchen. Remember how the hall carpet gushed under our feet? And how the dining room rug was so wet that impressions remained long after we stepped off it? What the hell were we thinking?

STEVEN

We survived.

MAN

What we did should have gotten you sent to boarding school, and me and Ira grounded until college.

STEVEN

My mom hardly noticed.

MAN

I don't know how.

STEVEN

Guess we did a good job cleaning up. All the towels and fans. When she got home after work she pointed to a dark spot on the rug and asked me what happened. I told her Ira spilled a glass of iced tea.

MAN

And she said nothing else?

STEVEN

Does it matter now?

MAN

No, of course not.
                    (a beat)

19

We were lucky.

                         STEVEN
Sometimes you have to be...
                    (a long beat)
I miss that house.

                         MAN
I do, too.

                         STEVEN
I miss it a lot.

                         MAN
We had a lot of good times there.

                         STEVEN
Ever drive by?

                         MAN
                    (he nods)
Sure, sure.
                    (to himself)
Only rarely, though. I don't want to tell Steven. It isn't that I
don't like to visit 44 Spenser Drive. It's that on the few times I
did park across the street and stare at the house, I got an
unsettling feeling that somehow, some way, the decades
would strip away and I could see as it once was.
                    (a beat)
Steven's mother opening the front door for Chuckie and me.
She never seemed particularly happy but was a kind soul, I'd
always thought. We'd slip by her and follow Steven to the
kitchen where we'd polish off a canister of Pringles, or
ransack a box of Yodels.
                    (a beat)
Tools strewn along the driveway, and music blaring from a
cassette player. Steven taking his moped engine apart to
clean the cylinder heads and spark plugs, insisting it would
make him go a few miles per hour faster. Later, we'd hear
mopeds in the distance and, soon after, Preston and Kenny
would pull up.
                    (a beat)

After dark, with a light on in Steven's second floor bedroom window, all of us laughing and joking, waiting to chase down rumors of a party somewhere in town. Arguing about sports or music or who were supposed to be the easiest girls in our grade, then daring each other to call them on the phone.

                    STEVEN
So how is everyone?

                    MAN
Everyone?

                    STEVEN
Our friends. You haven't mentioned them.

                    MAN
I don't know.

                    STEVEN
You don't know?

                    MAN
I'm in touch with Chuckie and Lisa a bit. Their lives are interesting, yet ordinary. I saw Kenny and the others at the last reunion. Some look good; some don't. Laura's still hot. We caught up a little. I guess over time, things change. We all went our separate ways. Colleges and grad schools in different states. Some have families; some don't.

                    STEVEN
You don't hang out with them? Ever?

                    MAN
You don't really hang out when you're in your fifties.

                    STEVEN
Is that a rule?

                    MAN
More like, just the way it is.
                    (a beat)
We were all friends for a time. Best friends. But then you

                    21

meet other people and become friends. Then you move on.
And you repeat this, over and over.

                    STEVEN
Then tell me about you.

                    MAN
Tell you what?

                    STEVEN
About your life.

                    MAN
My life?

                    STEVEN
Yeah.

                    MAN
What do you want to hear? A lot of time has passed. Things
have happened, good and bad. Most I probably don't even
remember. So you want me to tell you about things like
where I've been, what I've seen, what I've done, what I've
missed? Honestly, what good would this do?

                    STEVEN
Tell me.

                    MAN
Why?

                    STEVEN
Just tell me.

                    MAN
                (takes a deep breath)
After high school, I went to college. A decent one, the one
my parents wanted. A few years after, grad school out in LA.
Ended up living there for seven years. Remember your
brother telling us about LA? Gorgeous girls. Incredible
beaches. Sunny and warm all the time. It was everything he
said it'd be.

(a beat)

But I came back to New Jersey. For my mom, in part. She's not in Short Hills any more. Had to move after the divorce. Lives a couple of towns over. She misses our house on Joanna Way, when she remembers it. I know I do, too. I see my sister often. We were close, then weren't, now we are again. You know, she had a crush on you back then.

STEVEN

(smiling)

Yeah?

MAN

I've got a close friend or two. Started a business. I work too hard. Should have more in the bank, but don't. It's not perfect, but I guess I could say I've built a life.

STEVEN

A life.

MAN

Yeah.

STEVEN

But how ARE you?

MAN

You asked me that before.

STEVEN

You didn't answer.

MAN

Told you I was good.

STEVEN

Now tell me the truth.

MAN

How do you know it's not?

STEVEN

I can hear it in your voice.

                    MAN
Why now?

                    STEVEN
Tell me.

                    MAN
How am I?
          (almost to himself)
How am I? Not sure how to answer that. Not even sure I
have the time to stop and think about how I am. Definitely
sure I don't want to analyze how I am.
          (but Steven is clearly expecting more)
I'm fine. Okay?

                    STEVEN
Tired?
          (the Man doesn't answer)
Weary?
          (the Man shrugs)
Feeling old?

                    MAN
Feeling old? Don't we all?
          (a beat)
My lower back occasionally acts up and my legs sometimes
feel heavy. And, yes, I'm sometimes tired -- very tired. I've
got a lot on my mind.
          (a beat)
But I doubt very much you really came to hear my problems.

                    STEVEN
Problems are boring, don't you think?

                    MAN
Now they are, I guess.
          (a beat)
Back then, they weren't, right? Back then, problems were all-
consuming, so that if things didn't go the right way the world
would fall apart. Did Veronica like me more than the other

24

guys in school?

STEVEN
Would we both make the varsity team next year?

MAN
Was my mom going to ground me because I tried to heat leftover lasagna in her favorite Pyrex dish and it shattered into pieces?

STEVEN
(smirking)
My bad. I told you to put it on the oven coils. Who knew you couldn't do that?

MAN
Would we stay best friends through senior year, and after?

STEVEN
Never in doubt.

MAN
(nodding)
Yes, yes...
(almost to himself)
Now I worry about making payroll, and watch dementia steal my mother's once-robust personality, and question if my fifty plus years equates to a lifetime, or does the fact that I don't have a wife or kids -- and, because of it, not much of a family to speak of -- mean my life is less equal to anyone else's?

STEVEN
You worry a lot.

MAN
Who doesn't?

STEVEN
Not me.

MAN
Of course you don't.

STEVEN

And you feel sorry for yourself a lot.

MAN
(looks at him, annoyed)
You don't understand.

STEVEN

What's not to understand?

MAN
Life isn't easy. It never is. No matter what age I am. But it's
definitely worse as I get older. Like there's this weight on me
-- the weight of being irrelevant in a world catering to youth.
And I see my mortality on the horizon and worry if I've made
my mark. I worry, too, if that has any meaning whatsoever.
(a beat)
Oh, Christ, why am I telling you any of this?

STEVEN

Because you want to.

MAN

Not sure why I would.

STEVEN
(shaking his head)
And life keeps moving along...
(a beat)
So you just go with it?

MAN

Not exactly.

STEVEN

Well, what it is? Are you in control, or aren't you?

MAN

You asked me how I am, and now I'm telling you. It's not all
bad, of course. I'm living.

STEVEN

You're living.

MAN

Yeah, I'm living.

STEVEN

Doesn't sound it. Sounds like you're doing the minimum.
Remember how Coach used to yell at us, 'Ladies, you're
going through the motions today. Get your asses in gear, or
you're all sitting the bench.'
         (a beat)
It's very disappointing.

MAN

Disappointing?

STEVEN

Yeah.

MAN

What is?

STEVEN

You.

MAN

Me?

STEVEN

You sound so passive. Kind of timid.

MAN

Timid? I'm not afraid of anything. I lived through the LA riots,
for Christ's sakes.

STEVEN

I'm talking about fearing being old.

MAN

Well--

27

                         STEVEN
                    (interrupting him)
I wonder, how often do you do something on a spur-of-the-
moment, without worrying about the time, or having to wake
up early the next morning?

                          MAN
Steven, have you been listening?

                         STEVEN
I have.

                          MAN
You haven't heard a thing I've said.

                         STEVEN
It's a simple question.

                          MAN
I'll repeat myself. I have responsibilities. I have problems and
pressures, and no, I can't just ignore them.

                         STEVEN
Why?

                          MAN
Why?

                         STEVEN
Yeah.

                          MAN
I have employees. Bills and mortgages. An obligation to my
mom. So, yeah, I consider the consequences of my actions
before I do just about anything. The innocence of being a
teenager is so far in the past I can hardly remember a time
when I didn't feel the burden of adulthood. I have to be this
way.
                    (Steven smirks)
Don't give me that smug look.
                    (Steven smirks some more)
Your question is naive.

                           28

                    STEVEN
I can see it in your eyes. You've lost it.

                    MAN
What?

                    STEVEN
Spontaneity. Impulsiveness.
                    (a beat)
Balls.

                    MAN
Balls?

                    STEVEN
Yeah.

                    MAN
You're grasping at straws. If that's the worst criticism you
have of me, then I'm not so bad off.

                    STEVEN
Wrong. You're letting people and situations and worries
dictate your life. You do everything as a reaction to
something or someone else.

                    MAN
I told you before, it's called being an adult.

                    STEVEN
It's called dying a little bit every day.

                    MAN
I'd be better off dying all at once?
                    (hurt spreads on Steven's face. The man
                    walks away, angry at himself.)
Goddamn it.
                    (to himself)
We'd all like to believe we're indispensable and irreplaceable
so that tragedy never touches us. But we're each just a
whisper in a universe of sound. If no one hears us, does it

matter at all?
>   (a beat)
The truth is Death has each one of us in its sights. Death is
close. Death is familiar. Death is ubiquitous. Every moment
of every day. Whether you turn on the television or
computer, read the newspaper, or get a phone call at home
with news that your best friend has been killed while riding a
borrowed -- and unfamiliar -- motorcycle.
>   (a beat)
I can feel the anger wanting to erupt from the dark crevices
of my mind where I'd kept the wretched raw pain hidden for
so long.
>   (a beat)
Steven, it's not my goddamn fault that some poor bastard in
a truck couldn't avoid you when you tried to cross Kennedy
Parkway, I want to shout. You always rode the razor's edge.
Thinking you were invincible. But you weren't. That
afternoon, you lost. We all lost. I lost.
>   (a beat)
I want more than anything to break out of the cocoon of
complacency that has entrapped me for so many years and
vocalize my frustration so that it would be no faint sound, no
tiny whisper. But what's the only thing I did do?
>   (a beat)
I held back a tear.
>   (to Steven)
Maybe if you had been less reckless you'd still be alive
today.

>   STEVEN

You're gonna put this on me?

>   MAN

Who else am I going to blame? How could you get yourself
killed? How could you let yourself be taken from all of us?
>   (a beat)
I remember one time you telling me, with unwavering
bravado, how you had narrowly escaped crashing a
motorcycle into a tree as it skidded out from under you on
the tight turn of a wooded trail. God, I can still hear the thrill
reverberating in your voice as you described every detail.
What you were seeing. What you were thinking. How it felt.

Making the whole damn thing come alive. You called it--

                              STEVEN
A victory.

                              MAN
Yeah, that's what you called it.
                    (a beat)
But it wasn't really.

                              STEVEN
It was.

                              MAN
That time, maybe.
                    (a beat)
And the whole damn thing pissed me off to hell. Not because
you almost crashed. Not because you showed no regret, no
reflection. No, to be completely cross-your-heart-and-hope-
to-die honest, it was because I envied that you found such
life coming so close to disaster.

                              STEVEN
Isn't that what it's all about, pushing the boundaries? The
boundaries that hold you back?

                              MAN
I don't know.

                              STEVEN
Man, what are you waiting for? It's all out there.
                    (pointing beyond the stage)
Why are you being so chicken-shit?

                              MAN
Ah, and there's the anger.
                    (a beat)
Again.

                              STEVEN
It's not anger. I'm not angry at all.

                    MAN
You used to be.

                    STEVEN
I never was.

                    MAN
Yeah, you were.

                    STEVEN
No!

                    MAN
Maybe you don't want to admit it, but you had a bombastic,
screw-the-world attitude that I never understood. It was like
you held a simmering rage towards someone or something
that made you take perilous chances.

                    STEVEN
What do you mean?

                    MAN
You always had to test Fate, didn't you?

                    STEVEN
I wanted to grow up like everyone else.

                    MAN
You had a death wish.

                    STEVEN
I didn't.

                    MAN
Would it be more accurate to say you liked to tempt suicide?
                    (to himself)
We never used the S word back then. We never
acknowledged that there might be issues compelling you to
ride the edge of tragedy.

                    STEVEN
That's bullshit.

                              MAN
So what was it, resentment for your parents' divorce?

                             STEVEN
Never bothered me. You know that.

                              MAN
Or the family secret that you had been the replacement child
after the death of your older sister Sharon?

                             STEVEN
Don't even bring that up.

                              MAN
Or maybe it's just that being a teenager is one hell of a
difficult time, celebrating the highest highs today, then
suffering in the deepest depths tomorrow -- and for some of
us it was much worse than for others?

                             STEVEN
I loved every moment with you guys. I lived every moment. I
wanted it to go on forever.

                              MAN
Did you?

                             STEVEN
Of course, I did.

                              MAN
I don't believe you.

                             STEVEN
What, you think you knew me better than I knew myself? Is
that what you're saying?

                              MAN
                     (a beat)
Okay, okay... I'm sorry.

                             STEVEN

                               33

Don't say, 'sorry.' You knew me well -- of course, we were best friends -- but you didn't know what it was like to BE me. You couldn't get in my head. No one could. Let me tell you about living.

                    MAN
You're going to tell me?

                    STEVEN
Yeah.

                    MAN
About living?

                    STEVEN
Yeah, about living.

                    MAN
Give it your best shot.

                    STEVEN
Remember when we took that midnight ride across Short Hills to the 7-11 on Morris Avenue to buy a Sara Lee pound cake?

                    MAN
That's it?

                    STEVEN
Remember how good it taste?

                    MAN
It was just a goddamn pound cake.

                    STEVEN
It was more than that.
          (a beat)
Jumped on our mopeds. In T-shirts and shorts. Warm summer air rushing by us. The hum of our engines. Nothing held us back.

                    MAN

34

Another unexpected memory. So simple. So honest. We
didn't care about the time, or how far it was. We just wanted
to be able to go when we wanted, and do what we wanted.
            (a beat)
And, yeah, that Sara Lee pound cake was damn good.

                    STEVEN
And what would your life's resume be without that? Just the
same routine of coffee and business meetings, where the
biggest thrill of the day would be knowing you're getting an
extra hour of sleep later that night.
            (a beat)
Got a nice car?

                    MAN
Sure.

                    STEVEN
With air conditioning and a stereo?

                    MAN
Of course.

                    STEVEN
Bet you don't even do that now.
            (a beat)
Or what about that Saturday in April when we stayed up all
night, listening to The Cars first album over and over,
figuring out how to fix what was wrong with the world?
Talked and talked for hours, until the sun came up.

                    MAN
            (laughs)
We were so earnest. And so naive.

                    STEVEN
Ever do that now? Just talk with a friend, not worry about the
time, or whether you have to cut the conversation short to
get to sleep?

                    MAN
            (almost sheepishly)

No.

                              STEVEN
That's the real tragedy.
                    (shakes his head.)
You haven't been living.

                              MAN
I've been living.

                              STEVEN
You call this living?

                              MAN
It is what it is.

                              STEVEN
You're waiting for time to expire. And don't kid yourself.
There's nothing after. This is it. You're given time. Some
number of years, months, days, hours, minutes. Who knows
how much. No one does. So you live. You forget about the
clock ticking. You stop bitching and moaning and worrying
and complaining and lamenting and you just live your life.

                              MAN
I know...

                              STEVEN
You say that, but do you?

                              MAN
Yes, I know.

                              STEVEN
DO you?

                              MAN
Goddamn it, I know!
                    (turns away in disgust at himself.)
This is what I've been doing for years. Going through the
motions. Do you have any idea what it's like to live your
entire life and then question what the hell you've been doing

for the past fifty-some-odd years?
>(looks at Steven)
Of course, you don't. Maybe you're the lucky one.

                        STEVEN
What happened to you?
>(the man shakes his head)
I remember this kid -- my best friend -- who was everywhere
that I was. Hanging out all hours at night. Doing stuff during
the day. Chasing after the girls we knew, riding our mopeds,
practicing soccer at the Pingry fields, shouting the words to
every Cars song. What happened?

                        MAN
I have no idea.

                        STEVEN
Why not?

                        MAN
You get so caught up in the day-to-day troubles. Checking
off what needs to be done. Did this. Did this. Have to do that.
And the next morning, there's a new list. And I try to get
those done too. And it goes on and on and on.
>(a long beat)
I'm tired... I'm just so tired.

                        STEVEN
>(steps up to the edge of the stage. He
>gestures to the man, then himself.)
It's been a long time.

                        MAN
It has.

                        STEVEN
Too long.

                        MAN
Yes, too long.

                        STEVEN

37

I have a final question for you.

MAN

Make it an easy one.

STEVEN

They're never easy.

MAN

I know.

STEVEN

I can't stay forever.

MAN

I know that, too.
(a beat)
It's time you ask.

STEVEN

Why has it been so long?

MAN

I don't know.
(to himself)
But I do know. Whenever I think about Steven it hurts with a kind of pain -- a cruel kind of pain -- I had never felt before or since. So I tried to bury the pain in a black storage trunk at my mother's place. A time capsule filled with everything that had been a part of my youth: Comic books, coins, high school newspaper clippings, baseball cards, trophies, medals, letters and notes from girls. Each is like a piece of the puzzle that made up my life back then. Most important among these essentials are the pages of my feelings in the immediate aftermath of his death that explain the pain I could never express adequately in voice. How a part of me was changed forever, and my innocence was shattered. How all of our friends were forced to confront the tragedy of a friend being ripped away from us at a time in our lives when we needed each other the most. Why did this happen? I don't know. It wasn't God's will. It couldn't have been -- unless God was a malevolent son of a bitch. It wasn't Fate

38

either. Every event has a purpose, nothing is chance. In the end, perhaps, it was Evil mockingly displaying the power, with one hand, to take the life of a kid and, with the opposite hand, crush the innocence of so many others.
(to Steven)
Guess it was just time to let you know that I'm okay. Perhaps not living exactly as I'd hoped, but here anyway. Maybe I'm still searching for answers.

STEVEN

You may never find them.

MAN

I know.

STEVEN

So don't look for them.

MAN

Maybe I just needed to say hello, and goodbye, one more time.

STEVEN

But you can't say goodbye to me. You'll always feel the pain. You can never let it go.

MAN

I know that. I was there at the funeral.
(a beat)
Seemed everyone from school was there. Tears in their eyes. Guys and girls. Some bawling. And when it came time, I walked shoulder-to-shoulder with Chuckie and Kenny and Preston alongside the casket holding what was left of you. So no one has to tell me about heartache. I remember the heartache. Heartache so overwhelming, I spent days afterward on the edge of nausea, alone at home, lost at school, unable to think about anything but how you died, why you died.

STEVEN

Why I died...

MAN

A question as haunting and confounding as any I would face
for the rest of my life. With no answer. No reasonable
answer. No comforting answer. The well-worn conceit is that
time heals all wounds. It's a foolish to believe such
nonsense. Thirty-five years have done nothing to diminish
my feelings about why you died. It remains a singular life's
moment when everything afterward was different, changed,
tainted.

    (a beat)

But I also refuse to allow the pain, the tragedy, the loss, to
take away from me the memorable times, too. When you
and I, and the rest of our friends learned about life together.
And we smiled, and laughed, and joked around. And we
cared about each other. That, too, stays with me. And is as
indelibly marked.

    (he puts a hand on Steven's shoulder)

It's been good to see you again.

    (Steven nods)

We had moments that I'll never experience again for as long
as I live. Our friendship meant everything to me. Everything.

    (Steven bows his head.)

It always did.

      MAN

We lived.

      STEVEN

Yeah, we did.

    (a beat)

You need to, again.

      MAN

    (nods in agreement)

I will.

      STEVEN

Never forget me.

      MAN

I won't.

STEVEN

Promise?
                    (he starts to walk away, then stops)
Promise?

                         MAN

I promise.
                    (Steven leaves the stage)
I close my eyes. For a while. I don't know if I cry, or even
shed a tear. I just know I stay in the sheer darkness of my
mind until it's time.
                    (a beat)
I'm tired and lonely and sad. But not totally.
                    (he stands)
I open my eyes. In front of me I see the light of what will be
the rest of my life. However it might unfold. Behind me, the
apparitions of a thousand memories disappear down a
tunnel, long and dim. I can't see anything specific. But when
I hold my breath, I can hear whispers of sound.

                       THE END